Peppa Pig

Tiny Creatures

Peppa and George are helping
Grandpa Pig pick vegetables.
Grandpa hands Peppa a lettuce.

Peppa can see something sitting on the lettuce.
"There's a horrible monster!" she snorts.

"That's just a little snail!"
says Grandpa.
"Grrr. Mon-sta!" says George.

George likes the snail.

Suddenly the snail disappears.

"Where's he gone?" asks Peppa.

"He's hiding in his shell," explains Grandpa.

"Grandpa! George and I want to be snails," says Peppa.

"Well," says Grandpa, "These baskets
can be your shells!"

"I'm going to eat up all Grandpa Pig's
lettuce!" laughs Peppa.

"Oy! Keep off my lovely lettuce you cheeky snails!"
calls Grandpa.

"And when Grandpa Pig shouts at me," giggles Peppa,

"I'll hide inside my little house!"

"Mon-sta!" says George.

Here are Peppa and
George's friends.
"Can we be snails too?"
they ask.

"Well," says Grandpa. "You could be something else exciting from the garden." "What's that buzzing sound?" asks Peppa.

"It's coming from that little house," says Suzy.

"It's a bee house," explains Grandpa.

"It's called a hive."

"The bees collect nectar from the flower and then fly to the hive to make it into honey."

"Hmmmm, I like honey," says Peppa.
"Let's pretend to be bees!
Buzz buzz buzz ha ha ha!"
"What busy bees!" laughs Grandpa.

Granny Pig has been baking bread.

"Would you busy bees like some toast?" she asks.

"Yes please!" say Peppa and her friends.
"With lots of honey!"

"I like being a bee because they eat lots of lovely honey!" says Suzy.

"I like being a snail," snorts Peppa, "because they eat all Grandpa's vegetables!"